Contents

NAZI GERMANY

HUMILIATION

The German Empire came into being in 1871. In the years that followed, it grew in power and wealth and its citizens were very proud of it. Then came disaster.

With the loss of almost 2 million young men, Germany was defeated in the First World War (1914–18). Afterwards, the Germans were humiliated. They had to admit that they had caused the war and were forced to pay the victors huge sums of money in compensation. Large areas of Germany were handed over to other states and the country was forbidden to have any significant armed forces.

A NEW LEADER

During the 1920s, Germany recovered slowly and painfully. Then, in 1929, another disaster struck. The world economy collapsed. Millions of Germans found themselves without jobs and many people were starving.

In 1933, the Germans rejected their traditional leaders and voted into power a man who promised to restore their past glory and prosperity. This man was Adolf Hitler, the leader of a Fascist party known as the Nazis. Hitler believed in strong leadership, fierce nationalism and, where necessary, violence. He swiftly removed those who opposed him, put Nazis in positions of power and began to re-arm the country. By 1936 the German economy was making a remarkable recovery.

COMMUNISTS AND JEWS

Hitler offered to explain the past as well as promising to make a better future. All Germany's ills, he argued, had been caused by Jews and Communists. He outlawed Communism and issued anti-Jewish laws as soon as he came to power.

Gradually, backed by government propaganda, life for Germany's Jews was made more and more difficult. By the beginning of 1937, about one-fifth of them had fled abroad...

CHAPTER ONE

THE GREAT DAY

It was raining heavily when the Guthmanns boarded the *Maid of Kent*. Nevertheless, Mr Guthmann insisted on stopping halfway up the gangplank. Taking his wife and daughter by the hand, he swung their arms upwards and bellowed in his native German, 'Praise God! This is a great day for the Guthmanns!'

Anna cringed with embarrassment. If her father hadn't been holding her so tightly, she might have jumped off the gangplank into the harbour below. The Guthmanns' great day, she reckoned, could hardly get worse.

An hour later, as the *Maid of Kent* lurched across the stormy Channel towards Dover, Anna realised she had been wrong. To begin with, she was bored stiff. Father had celebrated his great day with two large brandies and had fallen asleep in his chair. Beside him, looking anxious and lost, Mrs Guthmann sat knitting doggedly.

The one passenger of Anna's age, a red-haired boy with his leg in plaster, sat with his nose obstinately buried in a book. The thrum of the engines and the drumming of the spray on the windows was broken only by bursts of vulgar laughter from the men standing at the bar.

To add to her misery, Anna felt seasick. The queasy feeling had begun the moment they left Calais and started pitching and rolling in the south-westerly gale. The stench of cigarette smoke, scent, alcohol, stale vomit and disinfectant did not help. Nor did the sight of the ashtray on the table in front of her. It looked as if it hadn't been emptied for weeks. Each time the ship rolled, a little avalanche of ash and cigarette butts slipped on to the greasy table.

'I'm going on deck for some fresh air,' announced Anna, rising unsteadily to her feet.

Her mother looked up. 'Are you all right, dear?' she asked anxiously. 'Would you like me to come with you?'

'I'm OK, thanks,' Anna replied. 'For goodness' sake, Mum!' she added crossly under her breath. 'I am *twelve*, you know!' At the same time, she understood her mother's concern. After all, only a few weeks ago Anna had needed all the protection she could get.

The second-class passenger lounge had two doors, one on either side of the bar. Without thinking, Anna made for the nearer. After a couple of steps she realised she would have to pass through a group of male drinkers.

A flicker of panic passed across her dark eyes. Her thin, pale face tightened. She saw again the angry crowd around the school gates. She heard their shouts, their taunts, their curses...

A florid-faced man in a suit of coarse green tweed had noticed Anna coming and, with drunken gallantry, he cleared a path for her to the door.

I must not panic, Anna told herself. I must not panic. She swept her hair forward to cover a fading bruise under her left ear and walked quickly towards the door. As she reached it, the ship lurched violently, catching her off-balance and flinging her against the man in the tweed suit.

'Careful, my love,' he said mockingly, taking his hand very slowly from around her waist. 'You shouldn't go throwing yourself on to a man like that. He might get the wrong idea!'

Although Anna didn't understand what the man had said, she could guess the gist of it. With burning cheeks and guffaws of laughter echoing in her ears, she wrenched open the door and hurried out of the lounge into the cool passageway beyond.

CHAPTER TWO

GONE FOR EVER

Anna's sickness left her the moment she went out on deck. The fresh wind cooled her face and she took a deep breath to get rid of the smoke in her lungs. Then, after standing and enjoying the solitude for a few moments, she took off her hat, shook out her long black hair and let it stream behind her like the tail of a racehorse.

That was better!

Cautiously edging forward until she reached the rail, Anna stared out over the churning sea. She had spent all her life in Neuhof, a small town near Nuremberg in central Germany, and had never seen the sea before. Its power and the patterns continually forming and dissolving on its troubled surface fascinated her.

As she watched, Anna wondered about the country surrounded by sea that would soon be her home. What were the English like? She had heard that they were a cold, reserved people, which didn't sound very promising. Several boys she knew said they hated the English because they were cowards – when they were losing the Great War they had called in their American friends to help them.

Turning her head, Anna stared at the grey chalk cliffs just visible in the distance. They were like a wall placed there to keep her out. She wondered what she would do if the officials at Dover found a mistake in her papers.

'Don't send me back!' she whispered into the wind. 'Dear God, please don't send me back!'

Anna looked down towards the sea again and began thinking about the life she had left behind. She remembered the faces of her friends, and imagined them recreated on the shifting waters. There was Ingrid Mansfeld, her likeness caught for a split second in the tumbling spray! Monika, too! And Robert! And Hilda, smiling just as she had done before the accident...

It was a sad game. Like the sea-characters, Anna's real-life friends were also gone for ever. Nor would she see her home again, nor Klaus, her sleepy sheepdog, nor Mrs Seyler at the post office who always gave her a piece of chocolate and called her 'my pretty one' when she came to post a letter...

All these people and all these things – the heart of her childhood – she had lost. And why? Because evil men like Commandant Ruge had branded her, her parents and others like them 'enemies of Germany'.

As her headmaster, the kindly Mr Müller, had warned her father after that horrible incident by the school gate, 'If you don't take your family away now, Mr Guthmann, I dread to think what will happen...'

It was a wise remark and kindly meant, too. But it was also cruel in its honesty. It left the Guthmanns with no choice but to leave.

CHAPTER THREE

MISS TINKER

The Guthmanns were lucky because they had money and contacts. In December 1936, only a week after Anna's ordeal, her father had taken Mr Müller's advice. He sold the family home and transferred his money to a British bank. A month later, having paid the necessary bribes, the family had entered France by train and continued across the Channel to London.

England did not make a good first impression on Anna. First there had been the dirty ferry and the humiliating behaviour of the men at the bar. Then came unfriendly neighbours, unhelpful shopkeepers and the deeply depressing weather. Winter in Neuhof had meant clean frost and bright snow; in London it meant endless grey days of damp and darkness.

Anna's isolation was made worse by her inability to speak the language properly. Her parents, who both spoke reasonable English, decided their daughter should not go to school until her English was good enough for her to cope without difficulty. So she stayed at home with her mother in their expensive flat in Chelsea, doing the homework exercises set by her private tutor, Miss Tinker.

Anna had never met anyone like Miss Tinker before. In Germany her teachers had been stern, remote figures who took themselves and their jobs very seriously. Miss Tinker was quite different. She wore bright, eccentric clothes and smoked gold-tipped cigarettes through a long cigarette holder.

The first thing she said to Anna when they were alone was, 'Now, Annie, enough of this formality – you must call me Pru. It's my first name, you know. Short for Prudence.'

The remark, when she had eventually worked out what it meant, immediately lowered Miss Tinker in Anna's estimation. How could she respect someone who asked to be known by her first name, and a shortened version, too? And how could she learn from someone she did not respect?

Gradually, however, Anna came to see Pru Tinker in a different light. She was eccentric, yes, but far from foolish. Her motto was, 'As English is an illogical language, it is best taught illogically.' She had no time for learning grammar, therefore, and a great deal of time for conversation, reading the newspapers and debate.

As her English improved, Anna came to look forward eagerly to Pru Tinker's thrice-weekly visits. They began each lesson by going over one of the previous day's newspapers and discussing a story that took their interest. Anna noticed, however, that her tutor always chose a story about Britain, never elsewhere in the world. When she asked why this was, for once Pru Tinker looked taken aback.

'Do you really want to talk about what's going on elsewhere, Annie?' she asked cautiously. 'Even in Germany?'

'Ja, Miss Pru,' Anna replied eagerly. 'I want to talk about everything. If I am not talk with you, how will I know what happens in the world?'

The remark was true. Anna's kindly but elderly parents had decided that their daughter should start life afresh in England. Whenever possible, therefore, they deliberately avoided talking about their previous life in Germany.

When Anna tried to raise the subject, they answered gently, 'All that is gone, Anna, dear. Look to the future and forget the past.'

But Anna could not forget. The hatred in the eyes of the mob at the school gate still haunted her dreams. She wanted to know why they had turned against her. Anna wanted to try and understand.

So it was that Pru Tinker became more than a tutor. She became a friend – Anna's first English friend – and by listening to what had happened to her, Pru helped Anna come to terms with it.

Gradually, piece by piece, Pru Tinker learned Anna's story: the horrible accident, the lies spread by Commandant Ruge, the mob of swastika-wearing bullies that had greeted her after school, and the bravery of Mr Müller.

In early April Pru Tinker told Mr and Mrs Guthmann that Anna's English would be good enough for her to start school in the summer term. Pru had already discussed this with Anna, so it came as no surprise to her. Nevertheless, the thought of returning to school brought back many of Anna's anxieties.

'Are you sure they won't tease me?' Anna asked during their last lesson together.

'Tease you?' laughed the tutor, plucking a cigarette from a silver case. 'Why should they tease you, Annie?'

'Because of my English, maybe? Or because of my race?'

Pru Tinker raised her feet and draped them in a very unlady-like fashion across the arm of the sofa. 'Your English is fine, Annie,' she declared confidently. Kicking off her shoes, she continued, 'As for your race – there are people from every race under the sun in London. The fact that you are Jewish won't even be noticed.'

'You are sure?' asked Anna.

'Of course! Lady Anne Spencer's College is one of the best schools in London, in the whole country, for that matter. Lots of foreign diplomats send their children there, so they're used to people from different backgrounds. You'll love the place, I promise you.'

CHAPTER FOUR

'ALL THE ANSWERS'

On arriving in England, Mr Guthmann had set up his own business in London. It was here that he had heard of Lady Anne Spencer's College for Young Ladies and decided that, whatever it cost, Anna should go there. 'It will make a real English lady of her, my dear,' he told his wife with a chuckle. 'Who knows, maybe one day she will be invited to Ascot with the king!'

Pru Tinker had also heard a great deal about Lady Anne Spencer's College for Young Ladies. It had a reputation for turning out independent-minded young women able to hold their own in what was then a man's world. This was why Pru had described it as one of the best schools in the country. Had she visited the place, however, she might not have been so eager in her praise. And she would certainly not have promised Anna that she would be happy there.

Lady Anne Spencer's – or 'Lassie's' as it was popularly known – was less concerned with pupils' happiness than with making them tough and independent.

'After five years at Lassie's,' the headmistress, Dr Amelia Forbes, was fond of saying, 'my girls are ready for anything – from trousers to tigers!'

• • • • •

Anna missed the first few days of the summer term because her mother kept her at home, nursing a cold. She was, therefore, the odd one out in her class, Remove B, even before she set foot in the school. When, a week into term, her mother escorted her through the College's imposing red brick entrance, Anna's heart sank. Everyone else seemed so assured, so confident.

Her spirits sank even lower when, during a brief interview, Dr Forbes suggested she change her surname to Goodman. 'Just in case,' the headmistress explained.

In case of what, Anna wondered, but said nothing.

After saying goodbye to her mother, Anna was escorted round the school by a tall girl with hard, Arctic blue eyes.

'I'm Barbara Dobbs-Barker,' she announced in a confident, upper-class accent. 'Expect you know the name.'

Anna smiled nervously. 'Yes. I've heard the name Barbara…'

'Not *Barbara!*' snorted her guide. '*Dobbs-Barker.* You must have heard of Daddy, the famous MP.'

Anna felt deeply uncomfortable. 'I am sorry, Barbara. I do not know him.'

Barbara seemed not to hear. They had made their way to the middle of a large courtyard. Waving her strong-as-a-hockey-stick arm in several directions at once, Barbara announced briskly, 'Gym's over there, netball courts behind you, science block to the left, history over it, Ma Forbes' lair over the archway, chapel's the building with knobs on, tuckshop next to it and all the other classrooms scattered about all over the place. Got it?'

Determined not to be overpowered, Anna said firmly, 'No, Barbara, I have not got it. Repeat, please.'

'Rrr-repeat? *Rrr-repeat?*' sneered Barbara, mocking Anna's accent. 'Where do you come from, Anna Goodman?'

Anna took a deep breath. 'I come from Germany.'

The statement had an extraordinary effect on Barbara Dobbs-Barker. Her shoulders relaxed, her lips bent into a smile and she pushed her grey school hat back from over her eyes.

'Germany!' she exclaimed. 'How jolly exciting! Daddy will be thrilled. You see, he really admires you people. He thinks your Hitler chap has got all the answers…'

Anna stopped listening. All the answers… Yes, maybe Hitler did have all the answers. He certainly had the oldest answer – blame someone else. Blame a minority, blame those who can't easily defend themselves.

Blame the Jews.

If Barbara Dobbs-Barker had asked Anna what she thought of Hitler, she would have given an honest answer. But as the MP's daughter was too arrogant to imagine anyone disagreeing with her, she did not ask and Anna held her tongue. When the time came, she decided, she would speak out. But not before.

In the meantime, it was quite useful being under the wing of Barbara, Remove B form captain, captain of the Removes' hockey team and winner of the Hornby-Williams Debating Cup. It meant you didn't get picked on.

Winnie Mickleby, who sat at the desk next to Anna's, was definitely not part of the Dobbs-Barker set-up. A quiet, sandy-haired girl with a round, dimpled face, she preferred reading to games, and music to debating. She was genuinely kind, however, and soon identified Anna as a possible friend and ally.

'Are you really in with Barbara D-B?' she asked timidly one break-time.

'Barbara is calling me her chum,' Anna replied cautiously. 'But I do not think she is meaning it. She does not really know me.'

'What's your secret?' teased Winnie.

'If I tell you, it is not a secret, is it?' laughed Anna.

Winnie suddenly became serious. 'If I ask you something, you won't laugh at me, will you?'

'Not at all.'

'OK. Will you come to the cinema with me on Saturday afternoon?'

'Ja, I mean, *yes*, Winnie!' Anna cried, so happy that she forgot her English. 'Of course I will come!'

CHAPTER FIVE

THE GERMAN MIRACLE

Anna's parents, who had also changed their name to Goodman to avoid confusion at Anna's school, were delighted that their daughter had at last found a friend. Mrs Goodman spoke to Mrs Mickleby on the telephone and arranged for Winnie's father to call for Anna after lunch on Saturday and take the girls to the Gaumont Cinema in Fulham Road. The local paper showed that both the afternoon films, *Too Late the Bride* and *The Egyptian Queen*, were suitable for children.

Anna hardly recognised Winnie when she appeared at the front door of her flat. Dressed in a bright summer dress, with white sandals and with her hair pinned back with a pretty hair clip, Winnie looked years older than she did in her grey school uniform. She seemed a lot more relaxed, too.

'I like your frock,' Anna said when they were safely seated in the back seat of the Micklebys' car. 'Is it new?'

'Yes,' Winnie explained. 'I'd grown out of last year's summer clothes so Mummy bought me some more. I like this one best. A bit different from school rags, isn't it?'

'You bet!' exclaimed Anna, whose spoken English was getting better every day. 'I hate uniforms!'

'So do I!' chimed Winnie. 'Did you have to wear a uniform before you came to Lassie's, I mean at your German school?'

Anna had never spoken to Winnie about her past and she was not sure that she wanted to now. 'We were not having to wear uniforms,' she said carefully. 'But some people did so.'

Winnie looked puzzled. 'Why only some people, Annie?'

'Please, Winnie, not now,' Anna replied, trying not to sound cross. 'One day we will talk about it, OK? But not now.'

'All right, Annie,' Winnie agreed. 'Let's forget about stupid uniforms – at least until Monday!'

● ● ● ● ●

Unfortunately, the subject of uniforms could not be set aside so easily. After sitting through *Too Late the Bride* – a rather soppy comedy about a woman who missed her wedding because her bridal dress got tangled in a lift door – the girls bought a Neapolitan cornet each and settled back to watch the newsreel.

It began with a long piece about the coronation of King George VI. Then there was something Anna didn't understand about Neville Chamberlain becoming prime minister. This was followed by a special feature entitled: *The German Miracle.*

Anna gripped the arms of her chair as pictures of new roads, smiling factory workers and prosperous shoppers flashed across the screen. Then came shots of seemingly endless columns of marching soldiers and Chancellor Adolf Hitler ranting at a huge crowd gathered beneath swastika flags.

Anna began to feel very hot. The air inside the cinema was so stuffy... it was difficult to breathe...

'Even boys and girls as young as ten,' the newsreader announced, 'have a part to play in the new Germany.' The screen filled with smiling mothers dressing young, blonde-haired boys in Hitler Youth uniforms. 'Yes, there's no doubt about it, Chancellor Hitler's Nazis have certainly managed to restore the Germans' pride in their native land!'

Stern-faced teenage boys in Nazi uniform marched past the camera singing a popular patriotic song.

'Unfortunately,' the newsreader went on, speaking in a deeper, more serious tone, 'there is another, less attractive side to the German Miracle.'

Anna stared hard at the screen. She knew what was coming next.

'There are a growing number of reports that in some towns and cities the Nazis are turning a blind eye to unruly behaviour. Jews, in particular, are being mistreated…' A shaky piece of newsreel showed a crowd of youths, all wearing swastika armbands, jostling a Jewish rabbi in the street. The man was pushed to the ground and the Nazi yobs began kicking him…

Anna could stand no more. Muttering to Winnie that she had a headache, she stood up and walked quickly out of the cinema. Seconds later, Winnie joined her on the street outside.

'What's the matter, Annie?' she asked urgently, putting an arm round her friend's shoulder. 'Hey, you're crying! What is it?'

'I'm sorry!' sniffed Anna, reaching in her pocket for a handkerchief. 'I was feeling ill… It was so hot in there!'

Winnie was not convinced. 'Hot? It's a lot warmer out here, Annie. Are you sure it wasn't the film, the one about Germany?'

Anna lifted her tear-stained face and looked Winnie full in the face. 'Yes. I should not lie. It was the film, Winnie.'

'What was wrong with it? Did it make you feel homesick?'

Anna gave a little laugh. 'Homesick? Yes, I miss some things. But no, I am not homesick for what I saw.'

'You mean those Hitler Youth people? And attacking that Jewish man?'

'Yes, I mean that, Winnie.' Fresh tears welled up in Anna's eyes and she clutched her hands together to stop them shaking. 'You saw the man, the rabbi? How they knocked him down? They did that to me, Winnie! They did that to me!'

CHAPTER SIX

THE BULLY

Winnie was deeply shocked by Anna's story. 'I don't believe it!' she exclaimed when Anna explained how Commandant Ruge had spread rumours about her and ambushed her at the school gates.

'But you *must* believe it!' cried Anna. 'These things are terrible, Winnie, but they are true! Look!'

Anna opened her mouth and pointed to a gap in her teeth on the left-hand side of her mouth. 'Two teeth are gone,' she explained. 'And it was not the dentist that removed them.'

'But that's awful! What about the police, what did they do?'

Anna sighed. 'Nothing. They are too frightened of the Fascists. Everyone is too frightened.'

'And just because you are Jewish, Annie?'

'Yes. Just because of my birth, my religion.'

The two girls talked together for another twenty minutes before going back into the cinema to catch the second-half of *The Egyptian Queen*. As they went in, Anna made Winnie promise not to tell anyone at school what she had learned.

'But why?' Winnie complained. 'It's really bad! Everyone should know!'

35

Anna frowned. 'One day they will know. But not now. Some girls in our class repeat their parents' words like parrots – you know, about the Fascists sorting things out. They think they like the Nazis and want them here in England.'

'Not on your nelly!' snorted Winnie.

'No! And not on yours, either!' grinned Anna.

• • • • •

At half-term Barbara Dobbs-Barker discovered that Anna was Jewish. It happened when she casually told her father that a German girl called Anna Goodman had joined her class.

'*Goodman?*' grunted the MP. 'Sounds like a Jew to me! Probably run away because old Adolf has made things too hot for her! He's fed up with their money-grubbing, y'know – can't say I blame him!'

When Barbara asked Anna if what her father had said was true – that she was a Jew who had run away from the Nazis – Anna did not deny it.

'Come to take our money, now?' sneered Barbara. 'Well, you're not welcome here!'

For the next few weeks, until she found a new victim, Barbara did her best to make Anna's life a misery. Barbara and her allies, Rosemary Pickett-Smith and Clarissa Claridge, called Anna racist names like 'Yid' and 'Jew-baby', barged into her in the corridors, borrowed her sports clothes (and never gave them back) and spilt ink on her books – accidentally, of course.

Winnie begged Anna to tell their young form mistress, Miss Garside, what was going on. But Anna refused. It would not do any good, she explained. The only way to stop the bullying was to change the way that Barbara and her friends thought.

CHAPTER SEVEN

THE TIME IS RIGHT

In the last week of term, when exams were over and teachers were struggling to find ways of keeping their classes interested, Miss Garside suggested a class debate. She knew the idea would appeal to Barbara Dobbs-Barker and reckoned the rest of the class would probably follow her lead.

Miss Garside was right. Because she was a good debater (and liked the sound of her own voice), Barbara declared the idea 'absolutely topping'. The rest of the class agreed – or kept quiet. The next question was what topic to debate. Miss Garside proposed the abdication of King Edward VIII, but she was voted down by a group of girls who wanted to discuss whether married women should go out to work.

Then Barbara Dobbs-Barker chimed in, saying that both the topics were 'old hat'.

'I vote we debate something modern,' she declared, 'such as "Fascism is the key to a better future".' She chose this topic because her father had been asked to defend the same motion in a debate at his old university.

Support for the other topics quickly melted away. Barbara's motion was accepted and she was chosen as the first speaker in its favour, supported by Clarissa Claridge. It was now the turn of those who opposed the motion to find a pair of main speakers. As Barbara glared triumphantly round the class, no one stepped forward.

'Come on!' urged Miss Garside. 'It's a very controversial motion. Surely not everyone agrees with it?'

Winnie glanced at Anna, nodded, and slowly raised her hand.

'Yes, Winnie Mickleby? Would you like to speak against the motion?' At the back of the class, Rosemary Pickett-Smith sniggered loudly.

'I wouldn't mind, Miss Garside,' replied Winnie shyly, 'but I'd rather be the second speaker. There's someone who'd do the main speech much better than me.'

'Yes?'

'Anna Goodman, Miss Garside.'

There were more snorts of laughter from the back of the class. After Miss Garside had quietened the girls down, she looked at Anna and asked kindly, 'Well, Anna, would you like to oppose the motion, "Fascism is the key to a better future"?'

Before she answered, Anna turned round and stared straight at Barbara Dobbs-Barker for a few seconds. Then, speaking very calmly, she said, 'Yes, Miss Garside. I would like to speak against that motion. I think the time is right, now.'

• • • • •

CHAPTER EIGHT
ANNA'S STORY

A whole Tuesday afternoon was set aside for the debate. Barbara Dobbs-Barker spoke first. Her father had armed her with impressive facts and figures to support her argument. For example, she asked, did Remove B know that under Fascism Germany's unemployment had fallen by fifty per cent, while Britain's was static or even rising? Barbara did not just rely on information. She knew how to mix statements with questions and how to raise or lower her voice at precisely the right moment. By the time she had finished, the majority of the class was convinced that Hitler's Germany and Mussolini's Italy were paradise on Earth, and the sooner Britain adopted Fascism the better it would be for everyone.

Anna waited patiently for the applause to die down before rising and walking to the front of the class. She looked pale but determined, with no trace of the nervousness that Barbara and her friends had expected.

They were so surprised by her confident manner that they forgot their plan to heckle her opening remarks.

'I have no experience of debate,' Anna began, 'but I do have experience of the topic we are debating. Personal experience. So, if I may, I will begin by telling you a story.

'Last year, in the town of Neuhof, in the middle of Germany, there lived a girl about the same age as all of us here. She had many friends and was very happy. For the sake of argument, let us call this girl *Barbara*.'

One or two girls glanced nervously towards Barbara Dobbs-Barker. The form captain's face was a mask of concentration.

Anna explained how there had been a terrible accident one afternoon outside Barbara's school. One of her best friends, Hilda, the beautiful daughter of the town's mayor, had left for home without her homework book. Noticing Hilda's book lying on her desk, Barbara had hurried out of school with it. By the time she reached the school gates, Hilda was on the other side of the road.

Barbara called to Hilda and waved the homework book in the air. Without thinking, Hilda stepped off the kerb into the path of a speeding car. She suffered terrible injuries to her head and spine and died a week later without ever recovering consciousness.

The whole town of Neuhof was stricken with grief. How could this disaster have happened?

Why had the lovely, golden-haired Hilda, only daughter of their respected mayor, been so suddenly snatched away? The answer was provided by Wilhelm Ruge, commandant of the local Hitler Youth brigade. Hilda's death, he explained to his boys, was not an accident. It was murder – a typically clever Jewish plot.

Who had found Hilda's homework book? Ruge asked. Answer: Barbara. Who had waved that book in the air, tempting Hilda to cross the road in front of a car? Answer: Barbara. And what race were Barbara and all her family? Answer: Jews.

What further evidence did anyone want?

Of course Commandant Ruge was talking nonsense. But in Fascist Germany, Anna explained, nonsense was often believed. The Germans wanted a reason for their humiliating defeat in the First World War and the terrible hardships of the depression. Hitler gave them a wickedly simple reason: all their suffering was the fault of Jews and Communists. The Communists were in Russia and could not be got at, but millions of Jews lived in Germany itself…

Day after day the anti-Jewish message was rammed home in schools, on the radio and in the newspapers.

In time even decent people began to believe it. So when, about a fortnight after Hilda's death, Commandant Ruge ordered his Hitler Youth brigade to line up outside the school 'to teach the murdering Jewess a lesson', even Barbara's friends were too frightened or too confused to intervene.

Terrified, Barbara walked slowly between the lines of angry youths. At first they just called her names and spat at her. Then someone threw a punch. Then another, and another. Barbara fell to the ground and covered her head with her hands. Kicks and blows rained down upon her...

Barbara would certainly have been killed if her headmaster, Mr Müller, had not rushed to her rescue and carried her to safety.

• • • • •

Anna, beads of sweat standing out on her brow, placed her hands on the desk in front of her. 'You understand, of course,' she said quietly, 'that the girl's name was not Barbara but Anna. That was my story. I came to England with my parents because my old friends had been taught to hate me. They hated me for my race and my religion. That is what Fascism does to people. I can never go home again. Now, Remove B, you must all decide. Do you hate me, too?'

Anna returned to her desk in absolute silence. For a long time no one said a word. Eventually, Miss Garside asked Clarissa Claridge to come forward and speak second for the motion.

Clarissa shook her head. 'I'm sorry, Miss Garside, but I can't. Not after what we've just heard. It wouldn't be right.'

Before Miss Garside could reply, Barbara Dobbs-Barker stood up. She looked unusually nervous. 'Excuse me, Miss Garside,' she began, 'but may I say something, please?'

Miss Garside nodded.

'I want to apologise for my speech,' Barbara continued. 'It must have been very painful for you, Anna. I don't think any of us knew what is really going on in Germany. Now, thank God, our eyes have been opened. For that we owe Anna our gratitude and our deepest respect.'

One or two girls started clapping. Barbara raised her hand. 'Hang on! I think the best way to show how we feel is to vote on the motion. All those who think Fascism is the key to a better future, raise a hand.'

No one moved.

'All those against the motion?'

The hand of every girl in the class shot towards the ceiling.

Anna, her eyes swelling with tears, stood up and said in a voice choked with conflicting emotions, 'Thank you, Remove B! Thank you for listening to me – and for understanding.'

• • • • •

NAZI EUROPE

ANTI-SEMITISM

Anti-Semitism is a form of racism. It means racial prejudice against Jewish people. The roots of anti-Semitism lie deep in Europe's Christian past, when the Jews were blamed for the death of Jesus Christ. Jews were also criticised because their religion allowed them to work as bankers at a time when Christians were not allowed to do so. Anti-Semitism was widespread in medieval Europe and was reinforced by the German Protestant leader, Martin Luther. Although anti-Semitism declined in many countries during the eighteenth and nineteenth centuries, it lingered on in Russia (especially), Germany and Austria. So when Hitler revived violent anti-Semitism in the twentieth century, he was heir to a long and shameful heritage.

ADOLF HITLER (1889–1945)

Born in Austria, Hitler left school without qualifications and failed to get into art school. As an embittered young man, he developed strong anti-Semitic views. He moved to Germany in 1913 and fought in the First World War, rising to the rank of corporal and winning the Iron Cross for bravery.

After the war he joined the Nazi Party and became its leader in 1921. More than anyone else, he was responsible for making racism a key part of Nazism. He set out his views in his book, *Mein Kampf* ('My Struggle', 1925–6). Nazi fortunes dwindled until 1929, when the effects of the Great Depression made Germans consider desperate remedies for their misfortunes. By 1932 the Nazis were the largest party in the German parliament. Hitler became chancellor the following year and immediately began to put his anti-Semitic policies into effect. These culminated in the horrors of the Holocaust.

FASCISM AND THE NAZIS

Fascism was a political idea introduced by the Italian dictator, Benito Mussolini. It opposed democracy and Communism and praised strong leadership and nationalism. Hitler's Nazi (National Socialist) party adopted Fascism from Italy. The Nazis' expenditure on armaments helped lift Germany out of its economic depression. This, with clever propaganda, gave the impression that Fascist Nazism was a desirable form of government. In the mid-1930s a number of important and powerful people turned a blind eye to the Nazis' evil policies and praised their achievements.

REFUGEES

Why did more Jews not leave Nazi Germany? Many did not believe Nazi anti-Semitism would last. They were, after all, loyal Germans who paid their taxes. Many of their parents and grandparents had fought for Germany in the First World War. Emigration was very expensive, too, and only better-off families, like the Guthmanns, could afford it. Finally, the Nazis made emigration difficult by delaying paperwork and charging high prices for visas.

THE HOLOCAUST

The Holocaust is the name given to the Nazi attempt to destroy all Jews living in areas under their control. Although the Nazis killed many Jews before 1942, the programme of mass murder did not become organised until that date. The most horrifying feature of the Holocaust was the establishment of death camps, such as Auschwitz, in Poland. Jews were transported there by rail, like cattle, killed by poison gas and their bodies incinerated in furnaces. More than 6 million Jews died in the Holocaust, perhaps as many as 4 million of them in Auschwitz.

CINEMAS IN THE 1930s

Cinemas were extremely popular in the 1930s. People went to see a whole programme of entertainment. This consisted of two films (a main one and a 'B movie'), newsreels, advertisements, trailers and, sometimes, another short documentary film.

New Words

Abdication When a king or queen gives up the throne.

Anti-Semitism Radical prejudice against Jewish people.

Commandant A commanding officer.

Communism A political idea, where all property is publicly owned. Today, only a few countries still have Communist governments.

Concentration Camp Camps set up by the Nazis for killing Jews and other 'unwanted' people.

Controversial Something about which there is disagreement.

Democracy A system of government in which power rests with the people and their representatives.

Depression The severe collapse of the world economy (1929–34).

Diplomat Someone who represents their country abroad.

Empire A group of lands under the government of one country.

Fascism An idea of government that emphasises nationalism and an all-powerful leader.

Hitler Youth The young people's branch of the Nazi Party.

Holocaust The Nazis' attempt to exterminate all European Jews.

Motion A precise topic for debate.

Mussolini The Italian Fascist dictator, 1922–1943.

Nationalism The exaggerated love of one's own country and intolerance of other peoples.

Nazi A member of Germany's National Socialist Party.

Newsreel A news film shown in cinemas before the invention of television.

Propaganda Information that is slanted to support one point of view.

Rabbi A priest in the Jewish religion.

Refugee A person driven from their home or country by war, oppression, famine or disaster.

Swastika A form of cross that was the symbol of the Nazi Party.

Yid A slang and offensive word for a Jew.

• • • • •

TIME LINE

1918 Germany defeated in the First World War.

1919 Germany forced to accept the Treaty of Versailles peace terms.

1926 Nazi Party sets out its racist manifesto.

1929 World-wide economic depression begins.

1932 Six million Germans unemployed.

1933 Hitler becomes chancellor of Germany,
Hitler introduces his first anti-Jewish laws.

1935 Nuremberg Laws take away German Jews' civil rights.
Many Jews flee from Germany.

1938 Germany united with Austria.
'Night of Broken Glass' (9–10 November): widespread attacks on German Jews and their property.
German and Austrian Jews sent to concentration camps.

1939 Second World War begins.

1942 Nazis begin their 'Final Solution': the attempted annihilation of the Jews of Western Europe (later known as the Holocaust).

1945 End of Second World War and the Holocaust.